WHO KILLED MY HUSBAND?

A short mystery

MICHELLE STIMPSON

CONTENTS

DEDICATION

For the One who makes life worth the living.
Christ.

ACKNOWLEDGMENTS

Thank You, always, to God for the talent to write and the gift of wisdom to translate His ways into fiction. I am constantly amazed at His lessons!

Special thanks to Tamara, Cassie, and Genea for reading advance copies and sharing your reviews. Thanks to all my advance readers! Woot Woot! Special thanks to Paulette Nunlee for sharing her editing gift. Thanks, Michelle Chester, for your input as well. It takes a village to raise a book, too!

BEFORE YOU START READING...

Let me say THANK YOU so much for purchasing this book! I pray it will be an entertaining, encouraging read for you. Be sure to visit me online at www.MichelleStimpson.com!

Again, many thanks!!!

Michelle Stimpson

1

"Thank you for doing this, Allan." I kept my eyes steady on the unfamiliar, winding road sprawling before me. Already, I had braked three times for sharp turns and a pothole.

Allan, ears covered by headphones, bobbed as though he didn't hear my compliment. His baby smooth skin, dimples, and semi-Mohawk haircut made him look much younger than thirty-two. So young, in fact, that a few times, twenty-something chicks at his DJing events had mistaken me as his older sister or his manager, even though I was only thirty. Allan thought that was funny. "It's good for business," he'd say, flashing his boyish grin.

I was tired of him acting like a boy. A guy. A dude. A bro. I needed him to grow up and be a man. Start thinking about things that mattered, namely his eternity. Since Allan had agreed to attend this non-church-affiliated men's retreat, I thought my prayers were finally being answered. I had gone all out to take off work early so I could take him to Peaceful Days. Even dusted on some makeup and flat-ironed my wavy mane so he'd have this awesome picture of me in the back of his mind all weekend.

I tapped him on the shoulder and mouthed again, "Thank you for doing this."

I knew better than to expect a "Sure thing, Ashley," or "It's my pleasure to go," from him. He was either ignoring me or caught up in a song. No matter, I was used to being blocked out of his life by music, working at KRBF FM radio Dallas. His side gigs. His friends. His lifestyle.

Still, my eyes watered for a moment. The rejection stung worse than a bee. At least when a bee stung, it was defending its own territory. Allan and I were supposed to be one in God's sight. Why he chose to turn on me—his wife of six years—and treat me like the enemy was unreasonable. We were on the same team.

At least we were until Corey died.

Blinking tears away, my vision cleared just in time to spot a pretty good-sized animal dart into the road. I slammed on the brakes. My stomach squirmed. I winced, hoping the thing had escaped being crushed.

A second later, my body relaxed. Whatever it was hadn't become a bump under my wheels.

"Geez Louise!" Allan yelled. "Can you not *see?*"

"It came out of nowhere!" I pointed toward the open field on the passenger's side.

"I saw it a mile away!" he claimed, motioning toward his window. "You're not paying attention."

"Neither are you!"

Allan pulled the headphones down so they dangled around his neck. "I'm paying plenty of attention to the road. Can't say the same about you since you nearly got us killed."

Cautiously, I continued our path to the campgrounds.

"Do you need me to drive?" he asked with a hint of sympathy in his voice.

This was my husband's way of apologizing. He wouldn't just come out and say, "Babe, I'm sorry. I shouldn't have yelled at you." He'd offer to do something.

"No," I said. That was my way of not accepting his roundabout apology.

I had grounds for a full-blown argument. How dare he accuse me of trying to kill us. And why am I driving anyway—I'm the woman! Real men know how to step up and take the wheel in more ways than one. Top that off with the fact that my heart was still racing from the animal-in-the-road scare, and I was primed.

But I didn't want to go there. Not now. Especially not today. Allan had finally agreed to attend a Christian men's conference for the weekend, and I'd been praying that God would use this weekend to touch my husband's heart. Having a big blowout of an argument just before dropping him off wouldn't exactly be productive.

Thanks to a few books I'd been reading and the personal advice of the Holy Spirit, I had come to the point of understanding that, apparently, Allan was in the "may be won without a word" category. I just needed to keep my mouth zipped and let God do His thing. Problem number one: Allan had a knack for provoking me. Problem number two: I wasn't always obedient. Problem number three: God was taking His sweet time.

My husband pressed a dial on his headphones. "Hello?"

The caller spoke loud enough for me to hear that it was a man. A hollering man.

"Wait up, man! I gotchu! My first payment isn't even due until next month, bro," Allan said.

I put two and two together and realized he was talking to Jerry Albright, the man who had helped finance my husband's acquisition of the radio station where he worked.

"I'mma have yo money *like* I said, *at the time* we agreed to," Allan said forcefully, slipping into a strong southern accent. "Why you tryna collect early?"

The rest of the conversation was much more calm. Allan wasn't playing with Jerry. But neither was Jerry playing with Allan, apparently.

Great. Now we have loan sharks after us. This whole DJ Pistol Whip persona was getting out of control.

"Aight. I'll talk to you next week. I'm gonna be at a...some kind of thing my old lady set me up to... Naw...you know I ain't goin' out like that! I got a reputation to protect!" Allan laughed.

Thank God they're laughing and not threatening each other.

Whatever the man had suggested was probably too civil for DJ Pistol Whip to admit to.

"I'll catch you later." He took the headphones off, mumbling to himself that Jerry was crazy. His thumbs whittled away at a message to somebody.

"In one-half mile, turn left on Prayer Lane," the navigation system instructed.

Allan chuckled. "Prayer Lane." He pushed his headphones back in place.

I could hardly wait for that half a mile to come and go so I could drop him off at that camp and burn rubber on my way out. I figured, if nothing else, at least I'd get a weekend away from him.

As we neared the grounds, we were welcomed

by the United States flag, the Texas flag, and the Christian flag. Flowers bloomed in pristine arrangements lining the entryway's white picket fence. Green grass rolled for acres between small buildings with country flair. A large pond sparkled in the midst of the camp. The scenery alone should have been enough to let Allan know that God is real and loves to bring beauty into this world.

Peaceful Days Camp was painted in bright red letters on a wooden sign. Underneath the facility name was the phrase. *Come all who labor.*

"That's what I'm talking about," Allan yelled. His music's volume must have been so loud he didn't realize how his voice carried. "Laboring is what I need to be doing this Friday night instead of hanging out with some chumps at a camp."

"Really?" I yelled loud enough for him to hear me. "You think judging a twerking contest is *labor*?"

"It's a hard job, but somebody's gotta do it," he shouted back. "DJing and vibin' with the hip hop culture is the way I make my money. You knew who you were marrying when you married DJ Pistol Whip, right?"

"I didn't marry DJ Pistol Whip. I married *Allan Crandall.*"

"One and the same, baby. One and the same." He bobbed his head even harder and started throwing punches in the air as though fighting an imaginary foe.

All I could do was poke out my lips. He had a point. Allan had turned into this persona he'd created to earn a living. He was very good at what he did. A part of me was glad that he loved his work. But when that work involved MCing wet T-shirt contests, I had a problem. A serious problem.

I followed the signs to the H. P. Lewis men's dormitory, which had been mentioned in the series of emails leading up to the retreat. Of course, all of the email messages came to me, since Allan wasn't about to keep track of anything regarding this event.

I parked and, almost immediately, Allan hopped out. I pushed the button to open the back window so he could retrieve his bags. As he walked around to the back of our vehicle, I got the paperwork from my purse. Suddenly, I felt like a mother must feel when she's dropping her child off at kindergarten. The joy. The pain. The pride.

A sadness swept over me as I wondered: *Will I ever experience that for myself?*

Thoughts of little Corey filled my mind, nearly overtaking me with their intensity. He would have been three years old the following week. "Horrible Threes" I'd heard people called them. People wouldn't say such negative things about babies and children—about them waking up in the middle of the

7

night, the crying, the teething, the getting into everything—if they realized what a blessing it was to have a living, breathing, normal, healthy child.

The tears had come too quickly for me to blink them away. I swiped them from my eyes.

Allan closed the back window.

I got out of the car to see him off. I had planned to give him a big kiss and a hug in Jesus's name, but I wasn't feeling my husband or Jesus at the moment.

Allan hoisted his backpack on his shoulder as he walked toward me.

All around us were couples saying goodbye. Hugging, slight pecks, praying with one another.

I looked up at him. Forced a smile. "Have a good weekend."

The heavy weight of concern crossed his face. "Why are you crying, Ashley? I'm at the retreat, okay? This is what you wanted, right?"

As mean as Allan could be sometimes, he always fell apart at the slightest hint of wetness on my face.

Peering into his eyes, I wondered why on earth God had allowed these crazy twists and turns in my life. My son's death. My failing marriage. Even my mother's dementia, which had been a long time coming, seemed an odd ending to such a good life.

If only my husband and I were on the same page, spiritually, I could lean on him. We could pray for each other. He could actually love me like Christ loved the church, and I could be submissive because I respected him, and life would be...well...easier and holier and basically better.

But I knew not to share my thoughts to Allan. No sense in talking to a brick wall.

Allan hugged me. "Get some rest this weekend. I know...." He sighed. "I know what today is."

"Yeah."

Allan still couldn't say Corey's name.

A tinny beat came from the headphones, interrupting our silent moment.

"Are you going to wear those all weekend?" I asked.

He shrugged. "I guess, when we're not doing anything."

I thrust the itinerary into his hand. "You've got a full weekend. There's no way you'll have time for music."

"There's *always* time for music, baby." He gave a charming smile.

I sighed. Twisted my lips to the side. This was a joke to him. If all he planned to do was go to the classes between vulgar songs, my efforts to get him here had been nothing but a waste of time, effort, money, hope, and prayers.

I blew a cool breeze from my mouth. "You're right. It's totally up to you, Allan. Enjoy yourself." I turned and opened the driver's side door, not wanting him to see my fresh batch of tears. I didn't want him to think I was trying to manipulate him by crying. Guilt-induced expressions of love were always disingenuous and short-lived.

Allan grasped my arm. "Ashley. Wait." He squared up my shoulders before I had a chance to wipe my cheeks dry.

"I'm here because I want to be here." He swallowed. "I'm tired of fighting with you. I can't change what happened. I can't fix everything like I want to. And I don't know God like you want me to. But I'm here this weekend because I *do* care."

"If you care, then *listen*. Take off your headphones and *listen* to what's in *here*." I placed my hand on his heart.

Slowly, my husband removed the black headset. He put it around my neck. Smiled. "You could use some music this weekend, I bet."

I giggled slightly. "You're probably right."

He rested his forehead on mine. "I love you, pretty brown-eyed girl."

His nickname for me, based on the Mint Condition 90s song, still made me melt. I twisted my lips to one side, then gave way to a smile of my own. "Love you, too. See you Sunday."

The truth was: I loved Allan and I knew he loved me. But if God didn't fix him that weekend, I didn't know what I was going to do. We'd already tried counseling. Well, *I* tried counseling. Allan went twice and said it was a waste of time. I bought his-and-hers versions of do-it-yourself couples therapy-type books. Allan never got past the first few chapters. I was getting to the end of my strategies for improvement.

———

Friday night found me in bed crying as I flipped through pictures of our wedding. We were so happy back then. We had the rest of our lives in front of us.

Or so I thought.

Taking off the afternoon and enduring the tension with Allan almost all the way to the camp had taken a lot out of me. I didn't want to argue with my husband. I didn't want to be so judgmental. I just didn't know any other way to make him see how much he needed Jesus.

Rather than cry my eyes swollen, I decided to get up and do some work. I logged into my employer's system and began to edit and comment on documents the team had uploaded. If nothing else, I could at least find some success at work.

2

Celeste had warned me that the temperature in Zoccara's Italian Cuisine was always chilly. She knew me well. I didn't go anywhere without a pair of socks to keep my feet warm.

"Girl, you need to get your blood checked for anemia." She used to tease me when she'd come over to the house to care for Corey and found the thermostat set on seventy-nine degrees.

Since she was a nurse, I'd taken her up on the advice. Sure enough, my doctor recommended more iron. I had been a fan of Celeste's advice from that moment on.

The red and black shawl I'd packed in my purse came in quite handy as I waited for Celeste's arrival. I took in the intricate Tuscan tile on the walls. Soft lighting and wine bottle displays added an authentic feel to the restaurant.

"This place is beautiful, and so are you, girl!" I complimented Celeste when she arrived wearing a cute, white lace maxi dress with nude heels. She always looked so beautiful, even in scrubs.

"Says the woman who wakes up like this every day." Celeste returned the compliment as she waved across my face and clothes. "You look amazing!"

We fell into an embrace and her spiral-curled brown hair fell across my cheek. It was nice to smell the familiar jasmine and vanilla-scented shampoo. Some things didn't need to change.

"I've been in Dallas for almost fifteen years now and never even heard of this restaurant."

"Well, you gotta get out more," she recommended with a full smile.

Celeste and I hadn't been out much lately since she'd taken on a few new home health patients. Her work with critically-ill children and their families often meant odd hours and last-minute changes in her schedule. I never gave it a second thought when she had to cancel or reschedule our occasional girls' nights out because I remembered all too well the nights she had dropped everything to answer a frantic call from me.

Our friendship had begun when the doctors said there was nothing more they could do for Corey in the hospital. Despite the surgeries and medications, they couldn't get ahead of the fluid building on his brain, called hydrocephalus. So much damage had been done already, they had come to the agreement that it would be best to put Corey on hospice at home.

Celeste had become our main home health nurse, helping to make sure his IV was properly rotated every three days, his feeding tube stayed in place, and nothing out of the ordinary was happening. She was very vocal about the fact that she wished the insurance company would have kept my baby in the hospital. "These doctors and hospitals have become so insensitive these days," she would murmur under her breath as we worked together to change Corey's sheets. "The whole system turns people into numbers."

I couldn't argue. As a mortgage analyst, my field was probably one of the worst when it came to taking people's individual situations into consideration. I understood all too well that businesses needed to make money, and doing so meant minimizing risks, maximizing profit. There were a few times I wanted to go to bat for someone, but my job had been so good to me—giving me all the time off I needed, even working with the IT department to set up a network so I could work from home in Corey's final weeks of life—I didn't rock the boat much. Shame on me, I knew, but I was just trying to keep putting one foot in front of the other back then. Buyers could get another house, but I could never get back those days with my son.

Celeste had been with me the night Corey took his last breaths. As much as I'd dreaded that day, Corey's passing had actually been peaceful. He looked like a little sleeping angel. My heart was torn to pieces, yet there was a quiet sweetness to the moment. Gave the word "passing" a different meaning. It wasn't a violent transition. Just his soul leaving his little body, as though it was simply the best time for him to return home.

Celeste had hummed a song that night, one with a moderate tempo. One I had never heard before, which wasn't a surprise since I didn't grow up in church. The song was not too slow, not too fast. "When we all get to heaven, what a day of rejoicing there will be." I found myself rocking to the beat long after the funeral home had taken Corey's body away. Celeste slept in the guest room. Allan was trying to get a flight back from New York, but he wasn't able to get out because of the weather. As much as I needed Allan, I was almost glad he wasn't there, because I'd needed to fall completely apart alone in my bedroom with just me and God. That's what I did.

And so did Celeste. I'd heard her. She'd heard me.

And before long, we teamed up and decided to cry together in the living room. That was when I found out how strong Celeste's faith really was. I'd never seen anyone praise in the middle of sadness before the night Corey died. It was beautiful, as though the Comforter Himself came and sat down in the middle of it all with us.

I didn't care what the protocol, I wasn't going to say goodbye to Celeste just because my son had gone home to be with the Lord. She'd been such a blessing to me. I needed her friendship, and she was more than glad to give it.

She didn't talk much about her subsequent patients. I didn't ask questions, either. Instead, when we caught up to one another, we focused on encouraging one another. Like sisters. In fact, Celeste and I had grown so close while caring for Corey, I never bothered to take back her key to my house. My family lived several states over and Allan's family was two hours away. If there was ever a time one of us got locked out of the house or if we were on vacation and something was happening with our residence while we were away, there was no one else I trusted to enter except Celeste.

"Ladies, your booth is ready," the hostess said, breaking up our hug.

We looped elbows and followed the young

woman, giddy with the unspoken excitement of being reunited with a dear friend.

We scooted onto our seats as the hostess gave us our menus. "Your server, Marissa, will be with you shortly."

"Thank you," Celeste said.

As soon as we were alone again, I could see from the extra-wide smile on her face and the cheeks pushed up so high that her eyes were nearly closed that Celeste was about to burst with news.

"Okay...what's up with you?"

She flashed her left hand, which sported a thin gold band with three diamonds.

"You're engaged!" I nearly screamed.

"Uh huh." She nodded.

We both raised our hands and clasped them high above the table, letting out little squeals of delight. We'd drawn a bit of attention to ourselves with this celebration.

"Calm down," Celeste warned.

We leaned in. "I can't! I'm so excited for you! Tell me all about him. And exactly when did you have time to fall in love?"

After we gave our orders to Marissa, Celeste filled me in on the whirlwind romance she'd been in with a man named Steve for the last three months, a man whom she'd met at her nephew's college graduation ceremony. Steve's youngest brother was receiving his degree as well.

"At first, I mean, I noticed him sitting next to me. He is cute, after all. But he was sitting next to a woman, so I didn't take a second glance. But then a man came and sat on the other side of her. And she kissed that other man. The man and Steve shook hands, so I was like—okay, he's not with her."

I nodded for her to continue the recount of events from their meeting, to their first trips to church together, to their morning prayer-calls and the roses he'd sent "just because." The beauty of fresh love.

I remembered it well. Try as I might to stay focused on Celeste's love story in the making, my mind took me back to the times when my eyes used to twinkle at the thought of my man. Allan and I didn't have a long courtship. When we met, we were both out of college, on good paths with our careers, and thoroughly enamored with each other. He was easygoing, and I appreciated that about him. We'd played enough games with people in our early twenties and didn't see a need to prolong our courtship or engagement. Being the decisive, take-charge person I've always been, I said "yes" when he asked me and it was a done deal. I wasn't a "wedding" person and I'm definitely not one to waste money. We had a small private ceremony at my parents' church—much to his family's chagrin. They'd wanted to go all out for their baby boy and turn it into a socialite event in their mid-sized East Texas town. But I wasn't having it and, truthfully, Allan didn't want it, either—though he didn't voice his opinion loudly enough, if you ask me.

"Ashley?"

"Huh? Oh! Yeah. That's great, Celeste. I'm so happy for you." I suddenly tried to find my manners.

"Will you?"

I didn't know what she'd asked me, but there was no way I could say no to Celeste, regardless. "I sure will!"

"Thank you!" she gushed. "I'll be sure not to put you in some crazy dress you'd never want to wear again."

I swallowed hard as I realized I'd just agreed to be in Celeste's wedding. This was a good surprise.

Marissa set a plate of jumbo crab cakes on our table. Celeste said the prayer and then we dove in.

"Enough about me. What's up with you? How's Allan? What's this men's retreat all about?" she asked.

I took a deep breath and a bite of food. I didn't want to tell her that things between Allan and I hadn't been going so well lately, especially not in light of her good news. I didn't want to discourage her about marriage in any way.

"We're good. For the most part. Allan just signed a deal to buy the radio station."

Celeste's eyebrows leapt. "Oh wow! That's major! He's gonna be, like, one of the most powerful men in the city. All the young people listen to that station."

"Yeah, it's a pretty big deal. He and Michael Rivers, A-K-A DJ Drop-the-Bomb, went in together. They've got some pretty big ideas about the direction they'd like to see things go." I took another bite of food.

"You don't seem very happy about it."

I swallowed. "You know, I want the best for Allan. I really do. And I don't want to seem judgmental..."

"But," Celeste said.

"But," I continued, "have you ever *listened* to KRBF?"

She shook her head. "No, but I know what they play. And you're right. You are being judgmental. Owning a radio station is just a job. Not everyone has the luxury of nursing or helping people buy homes responsibly." She'd pointed to herself and then to me. "Allan is in a supply-and-demand job. Artists supply music that people demand. It's that simple. Besides," she smiled and snapped her finger, "you just got saved, like, five minutes ago. You cannot be this judgmental this fast. You gotta grow up in the church and start wearing long skirts before you can do that."

"It's just so..." I tried to explain through laughing

at her joke, "when he would listen to the station while we're riding somewhere, the music was so offensive. Filthy. I mean, I get that he was trying to listen to the station for business purposes. He wanted to make sure the commercials aired at the right time and completely. He wanted to hear what new DJs were doing so he could give them some pointers. I totally understand. But it's hard to sit there and *not* be critical when I hear the lyrics about people's body parts or what they're gonna do in bed and how they gotta kill anybody who stands in between them and gettin' that easy money. It's just…I insisted Allan start putting on headphones because I couldn't take it."

"What?"

"Girl, it was too much."

"You were the one always complaining about how he never took those things off. But you made him put them *on* when you two rode together?"

"I didn't have a choice!" I said, pressing my fingertips against my chest.

Celeste rolled her eyes. "Your ears are not going to fall off at the sound of a cuss word."

"But it's more than the words. It's, well…you just said so many young people listen to those songs every day. How can I be elated about the fact that my husband is on the cutting edge of promoting this detrimental gangsta mentality to the next generation?"

"Look." Celeste arrested me with a solid glare. "You are not Allan. Allan is not you. It's a free country. People are free to make money in whatever field they choose, so long as it's legal. You have to let Allan know that you support him, that you admire his drive to succeed, and that you're proud of his efforts to be a good provider for you."

I leaned to the side and rubbed the back of my neck. "What he's doing goes against my beliefs."

"But it doesn't go against *his* beliefs. And right now, Allan's beliefs and your beliefs aren't the same. You can't hold him to a standard that he hasn't agreed to abide by. And I really don't know if he'd agree with you, even if he *were* a Christian. Men have a knack for separating feelings from their work."

I peered at her. "How'd you get to know so much about men, Miss-I'm-thirty-and-just-now-in-a-serious-relationship?"

"Ha, ha, ha," she jeered. "Don't try to change the topic. Anyway, if Allan's attending a Christian men's retreat, I'd say some things are about to change. This time last year, Allan wouldn't go near a preacher."

"Yeah, well, I'm not going to put all my eggs in the weekend-retreat basket."

"Ashley."

"What?"

"Stop trying to be Allan's savior. Just be his *wife*. Okay?"

I knew Celeste was right. Theoretically. Probably even biblically. But I had to take her words with a grain of salt. Or maybe I just chose to take them with a grain of resentment. Anger. She'd never been married. She didn't know what it was like to be married to an unbeliever, and I prayed she never would.

Thankfully, the server brought out our main entrees before Celeste could get into a really deep throw-down lecture. The delectable dishes gave us more than enough reason to switch the subject. We talked about other things—our jobs, her extended family, and of course her wedding plans. She pulled up pictures of dresses and table decorations. She asked for my opinion on floral arrangements and party favors.

We ended our time together on a high note, with a prayer for my current marriage and her upcoming nuptials. She kissed my cheek as we parted in the parking lot.

"Love you, Ashley. Don't spend so much time worrying about people. You gotta enjoy life, you know?"

"I know," I agreed. "And you deserve to enjoy yours, too. I'm so happy for you and Steve."

"And I'm happy for you and Allan. Don't give up on him, sis. You two have been through a lot. You're both still healing, recovering from Corey, really."

It seemed weird, but there was so much comfort in hearing someone say Corey's name. The way people avoided speaking of him directly sometimes made me feel as though they weren't acknowledging that my baby had lived. Hearing Celeste say "Corey" reminded me that someone else knew him, loved him, and hadn't forgotten about him, either.

I nodded. "Okay. I'll give him another chance. Since *you* asked."

"Don't do it for me. Do it because Jesus would do it for you."

Laughing, I said, "You like to roll up on people and do those Jesus drive-bys, don't you?"

She winced. "Jesus drive-by? Girl, you've been listening to too much gangsta rap. Startin' to sound like Allan!"

"Girl, bye." I waved at her and walked to my car, still laughing.

———

Though Celeste had couched her wisdom in humor, the message rode home with me: Treat Allan the way Jesus treats you. When I thought of His patience, His love, and how He had drawn me to Him in loving kindness, there was no way I could hold a grudge against my husband for not being drawn close to Him at the exact same time as me.

Instead of overdosing on movies, I decided to end the night earlier than planned and in prayer. Meditating on the name of Jesus pulled me down to my knees, brought me to conviction and repentance, and filled my heart with a renewed sense of peace about me and Allan. *Maybe God is going to use this weekend in a mighty way.*

I plugged my phone into the charger and set my alarm for 7:30 a.m., so I could get to early service and then go pick up Allan by eleven, the official end-time of the retreat. Then, I slipped between my sheets and fell asleep.

Until my doorbell rang at 6:57 a.m. I wasn't exactly sleep, but not in the mood to get out of bed yet.

I scrambled to my feet and threw on my robe. The only people who disturbed me at that time of morning were my new neighbors, whose puppy kept getting into my backyard somehow. I'd told them the last time that if Scruffy escaped, they had my permission to enter my gate to get him. But that hadn't happened in a while since the dog had grown too big to slip through the gate's iron bars. I thought to myself as I tied the terrycloth belt around my waist. *Maybe I should get a dog to keep Scruffy from coming onto my territory.*

To be safe, I asked, "Who is it?"

"Officer Logan."

A shiver ran through my body. Was this the beginning of an attempted home invasion, where the criminals pretended to be an officer in order to gain access to my home? I'd seen plenty of those chain emails on social media—maybe this was the real thing. My only safe haven was my bedroom, which I'd had built with no outside access.

I glanced out the slender window to my right. For a moment, I was relieved to see the police cruiser at the curb with the familiar city logo and a set of real lights atop the hood of the white Crown Victoria.

But then another reality hit me: *If the police are at my home, something bad is happening.*

I quickly opened the door, bracing myself for bad news and reminding myself that whatever it was, I could take it. I'd already lost a child, which I'd heard was the worst thing a person could ever endure. Allan and I had made it through that. We'd make it through this, too.

"Mrs. Crandall?" The tall, box-faced man asked. His much shorter companion tipped his hat.

"Yes. I'm Ashley Crandall."

"Ma'am, I'm Officer Logan. This is Detective Jackson. Dallas County Sheriff's Office. I'm sorry to tell you this, but there was an incident at the retreat. Your husband is dead."

3

"What? No. NO. Not *my* husband!" A scream vibrated in my throat. My knees buckled and I slumped to the floor.

This is not happening.

Both officers reached for me, but I kicked at their hands. "No. No. NO!!!"

"Ma'am, please let me help you up," Officer Logan said.

I was thinking that if I didn't let them touch me, this wouldn't be true. They would walk away and Allan wouldn't be dead.

They held out arms and I somehow managed to grab them. The officers got me up into a standing position again.

"May we come inside?" Jackson asked. His voice

sounded a lot like my father's. Soft for a man, yet soothing.

Why do these men want to come into our home? Instinctively, I thought that maybe I should wait for Allan before I let them inside. *But they just said he's dead.*

"Mrs. Crandall, we need to speak to you," Logan reiterated sternly.

"Wh…What's going on? What happened to Allan?"

"That's what we're trying to determine," Jackson said.

I gathered myself together enough to lead them to the couches in my front living room. Jackson clicked a pen and pulled out a notepad. I held on to my sides and began to rock myself to a slow, sad beat. *Allan is dead. Allan is dead. Allan is dead.*

"Mrs. Crandall, I know this is a sensitive time. However, time is of the essence. I have to ask you some pertinent questions."

I nodded.

"Do you have any idea who would want to kill your husband?"

"What?" The beat in my head stopped. "There was an *accident*, right?"

"No, ma'am. I said there was an *incident*," Logan corrected me.

"What kind of incident?"

"We're not exactly sure," Jackson said with a quick shake of the head. "Our preliminary thoughts are leaning toward homicide. We need to ask you some things about your husband. Again, do you know of anyone who would want to kill him?"

I closed the top of my robe over my neck. "Allan was a DJ. He did a lot of parties. He was popular across the Dallas area, so he had a lot of haters. Rivals. But no one who wanted him *dead*."

"Did he owe a debt?" Logan asked.

"Yes, he did," I admitted. "He just went in on a business deal to buy the radio station where he's worked for the past four years. He took out a loan at our bank for most of it. He borrowed the rest from a friend. Allan was paying the money back, though, so I wouldn't say that person wanted him dead."

"Who is the friend?" Jackson asked, with his pen propped.

Suddenly, flashbacks of recent run-ins between police and civilians flashed through my head. I didn't want the police harassing anyone unnecessarily. But then again—my husband was dead! "Jerry Albright. They went to college together. I can get you his number from his wife through social media, I'm sure."

"Can you get into your husband's email or social media accounts?" Jackson wanted to know.

"No. He's not really into social media. The people at

the radio station keep his accounts going for the most part. He pretty much handles email and other business on his phone. He only uses his laptop for music." In a moment's time, I realized I was referring to Allan in the present tense, as though still alive. *Allan is dead.*

"Have you checked his phone?"

"We've had to subpoena records. His phone was destroyed," Logan said.

"Destroyed?"

"Yes. In water."

I blinked hard. "Did he drown?"

"We were just about to ask you, Mrs. Crandall, could your husband swim?" asked Logan.

"Yes, he could," I said. "Why?"

"His body was found floating in a pond at the retreat."

"That makes no sense. Allan was a good swimmer. There must be some mistake." None of this was registering yet.

Detective Jackson took a deep breath. "I'm going to show you a picture of a tattoo from the victim's body. You tell me if it appears to be Allan's tattoo."

I nodded again. When I saw the black pistol tattooed on the wrist with Allan's DJ name underneath, my body froze. My Allan. Floating. Dead. "Yes. That's him," I managed to squeal.

"Oh God, please help me." I covered my face with

my hands. This was too much. A car wreck I could take. Sickness I could handle. But this was too much. The glass bowl of colorful marbles on my coffee table was the closest thing I could get my hands on so I could vomit.

Bile violently projected its way up my esophagus and into the bowl.

This is too much, Lord.

When there was nothing coming from my mouth except heaving, I excused myself to put the bowl in the kitchen. Jackson and Logan gave me the moment alone.

I returned to find them both engaged in their cell phones, perhaps scrolling through information from Allan's death scene.

"I want to know everything you know so far," I said.

Logan started, "We got a call around 4:20 this morning that there was a man floating in the pond at Peaceful Days. We arrived on the scene and retrieved the body from the pond. He was deceased. There were no signs of external trauma to his body. But his pants and shoes showed signs of being dragged, which leads us to believe that someone dumped his body into the pond after he was already unconscious. The coroner has his body. We need your permission to perform an autopsy."

"Yes, of course. You've already taken him away?" I asked.

"Yes," Jackson said.

That didn't seem fair. Wasn't I supposed to get a chance to say goodbye to him? "Why wasn't I called to the scene?"

"The fewer people we have present to contaminate an investigation, the better," Detective Jackson said. "I assure you, our team did its best to preserve your husband's dignity. Several people are still there examining the scene now."

My cell phone rang. "Can I answer that?"

"Yes," Jackson said.

Quickly, I rushed to my bedroom and answered the phone, hoping against all logic that it was Allan calling to ask when I'd be on my way. *These officers have it all wrong.*

I saw Allan's brother's name on the caller ID. Maybe Allan was at his house. *Allan probably got tired of all the church stuff and left the retreat early. That's why the officers couldn't find him.*

"Hello?" I answered.

"Ashley, what's this about Allan R-I-P on his Facebook page?"

My heart sank. The last-ditch theory of mistaken identity was blown. "Byron, something happened to—"

"What? It's *true?*"

"Yes, I—"

"And *this* is how his *family* hears about it? Facebook? What is *wrong* with you?"

"Byron, I just found out myself! I...I gotta go. I'm talking to the detective now."

"Detective? Wait—what happened? Did somebody kill him?" His voice cracked with emotion.

"Maybe. I don't know. I'm sorry. I'll call you back."

I ended the call and walked back to the living room with my phone in hand.

"Sorry about that. Family members are starting to call. The word is getting out, thanks to the Internet," I said, taking my seat again.

"It's quite unfortunate these days," Officer Logan said. "You might want to get someone over here to help field phone calls. Be a go-between for you."

Sounded like good advice.

"Mrs. Crandall, I must ask," Detective Jackson said, "did you visit your husband at all any time this weekend?"

"No. I dropped him off Friday afternoon and that was the last..." I couldn't say it.

"Where were you between the hours of eight p.m. yesterday and this morning at four?"

My chest tightened. I had to remind myself that the man was only doing his job. "I was out with my friend, Celeste. We met up for dinner at Zoccara's

33

in North Dallas. Then I came home and went to bed."

"What time did you arrive home?"

"Around 8:45."

"Do you have any evidence to corroborate?" he asked.

"Ummm...no." I racked my brain. If I had known I would be the subject of an investigation, I would have brought home a doggie bag. "Celeste paid for the bill. She's got the receipt. I'm guessing they have cameras at the restaurant, too," I shrugged.

Jackson scribbled more notes. "How can I get in touch with Celeste?"

Hers was one of the few numbers I had memorized, so I quickly gave it to him. "And may I have your number as well?"

"Certainly."

Once I shared my number, Detective Jackson clicked his pen again and stood.

Logan followed suit. His knees popped loudly. "Ooh! Forgive me for that. These old bones don't work like they used to."

All I could think of was the fact that Allan and I wouldn't grow old together. He wouldn't get to have popping bones and bifocals and gray hair or no hair. *Allan is dead.*

The detective gave me his card. "If you think of

anything, if you remember anything at all. If anything out of the ordinary happens, give me a call."

"You think I'm in danger?" I asked.

"I wouldn't say that," he clarified. "Just keep your eyes open for anything unusual."

I tsked. "*Everything* is unusual. Everything is *unreal* right now."

"It'll be that way for a while," Logan said with genuine sympathy. "You've got someone you can call to help you through? Family? Friends?"

"Yes. I do. Thank you."

"The coroner will give you a call. Probably sometime tomorrow," Logan told me.

"I can see Allan then?"

"Yes."

I showed the officers to the door. Once they were outside, I watched them through the side window as though watching a movie of someone else's life. They stopped in front of my SUV. Jackson bent down to look at my front driver's side tire. He pointed at something. Logan nodded. Jackson quickly took out his phone and took a picture of the front end.

Why are they taking pictures of my car?

They went on to the police cruiser and left me alone with my grief.

4

It's amazing how fast bad news travels. I could barely answer one phone call before my screen showed another call, then another, then another trying to come through. Text messages, instant messages, and email messages had my phone beeping and vibrating nonstop.

People wanted to know everything, starting with exactly what happened. When I couldn't explain that well enough, they wanted to know what was Allan doing at a men's retreat—that didn't sound like something he would do. Then they wanted to know who killed him. Did Allan try to fight for his life? How long had he been dead?

I finally just started saying I didn't know all the details, because it was the truth, aside from the fact that their questions tired me. Didn't they know how painful it was for me to repeat the same things over and over again?

Celeste finally arrived at the house around noon. She took over phone duty for me by sending every call straight to voice mail, except those names I had written on a list—my sister, my father, Allan's brother, Byron, or his mother. Everyone else would have to wait, including his job.

Besides, Byron was close enough friends with the people at KRBF. If Byron knew, they'd know soon enough. The whole world would know soon enough.

"Ashley, come lay down on the couch," Celeste instructed after my third bout with bile in the restroom. "I'll keep an eye on you."

"Shouldn't you be with that new family and their baby?" I asked.

"My shift starts at seven tonight. Your sister is flying in."

"Rae's coming?"

"Yes."

"Who's going to watch my mother?"

"Don't worry about that," Celeste said. "She's got it covered."

Like a child, I followed Celeste to the leather-cushioned sofa in the family room. She fluffed a pillow under my head and covered me with a Dallas Cowboys fleece throw blanket.

I closed my eyes, thinking surely tears would

come. Surely I'd start crying and screaming and falling apart. But I couldn't cry, not with all those questions swirling in my head: Did Allan get into an argument with someone at the retreat? Did a wild animal attack him while he was outside? He had roommates for the weekend—what did they say? *Who killed my husband?*

Aside from what happened, the aftermath brought even more questions: Why didn't the officers take me to see my husband's body? Did I *want* to see Allan's body in terrible condition? Were the officers holding back information because they thought I had killed my husband?

The lump in my throat wouldn't go anywhere, yet the tears wouldn't spring forth. Without answers, this whole grieving process seemed to be on hold. The worst question: What if I never got those answers? Would I ever be able to grieve if I never knew the whole truth?

———

I don't remember Celeste leaving or Rae arriving. The change of guards happened while I was asleep. I awoke to the sound of Rae giving someone a royal tongue-lashing.

"Look, this house belonged to Ashley before she

ever met Allan, God rest his soul. You will *not* disrespect my sister in her home. Not on *my* watch."

I sat up and leaned toward the front room, trying to decipher voices.

"We don't want no trouble."

I recognized that voice as Byron's.

Rae said, "Don't start none, won't be none."

"We're grieving, too, you know," from my mother-in-law. She sniffed.

"We're . *All*. Grieving," Rae enunciated. "But what you're *not* gonna do is come in here and fuss at my sister for what other people put on Facebook. She cannot be held accountable for the fact that some insensitive nut with no home training found out about Allan's death and posted before she had a chance to call you. Capiche?"

I rolled my eyes. *Rae, Rae, Rae*. My little sister had no sense of diplomacy. Couple that with her fierce loyalty to family and there you have it: a pit bull wearing designer perfume.

I threw my blanket to the side and kicked my legs off the couch. My feet landed on the floor just as my sister, Byron, and Allan's mother, whom everyone called "Honey" entered the family room. Their family resemblance to Allan—dimples, light brown skin, pointy noses—nearly caused a second collapse in me.

Honey ran toward me with a hug and a long wail. Her pain was nearly palpable. I wanted to take it in and feel it, too, but I couldn't. There was still too much to know.

Plus I hadn't seen Allan's body with my own eyes. That picture of the tattoo on somebody's wrist hadn't proven anything to my heart.

"Come on, Momma. Sit down." Byron coaxed Honey to a seated position.

Rae was next in line for a hug, since I hadn't greeted her upon arrival.

"How's Momma?" I whispered into her ear.

"Momma's fine," she whispered in mine.

I squeezed my sister tightly again, then stepped back to look at her. She was the spitting image of Mom in her younger years, except Rae's skin had a tinge of brown, courtesy of my dad's melanin. We both had wildly wavy hair, high cheekbones, and a sprinkling of freckles; we were often mistaken for twins.

Rae and I hadn't seen each other in nearly seven months due to my busy lifestyle and her taking care of our mother. She had all but sacrificed her personal life when Momma was diagnosed with dementia two years earlier. That was right around the time Corey passed. Rae took the reigns, caring for Momma, to everyone's surprise. I had always been the responsible eldest child, Rae, the wild baby of the family. But when I was in no shape to assume the duty, Rae stepped up without even being asked.

"Can Daddy handle Momma without you?"

"He's been doing it for thirty-five years now. I'm sure he can handle her for a week or so. Aunt Martha said she'd drop by every day. Make sure they eat, straighten things up. Doctor said it was okay to give Momma a little more of her sedative under the circumstances, so she won't have so much anxiety about me not being there. She'll be fine. I told her I was going on a shopping trip."

"Hmph. I'm almost *glad* Momma doesn't know what's going on," I said. "She thought Allan hung the moon, you know?"

"Don't I? She was always on me about why I couldn't find me a nice boy like Allan and settle down." Rae chuckled. "Enough about Momma. She's good. I'm here for *you*, Ash."

Byron spoke up. "So Ashley, what's going on? What are the police saying? When can we go see him? Where is he? What happened?"

I sat in Allan's lounge chair and filled everyone in on what little I knew. Honey cried softly, shaking her head. Byron balled his fist and planted it on top of his mouth. Rae crossed her arms and bit her bottom lip. I could tell she was trying in vain to connect the dots and solve the mystery.

"When will we know the results of their investigation?" Byron asked.

I shrugged. "Your guess is as good as mine."

"Nu uh," Rae said. "You need to go up there and demand some answers, Ash. Your husband is *dead* and those cops are probably somewhere eatin' donuts right now."

"Right!" Byron seconded. "Somebody killed my brother and I want to know who it is!"

"Don't you go gettin' no crazy ideas, Byron," Honey warned him. "Let the police handle it."

"They'd better, or else I will. This don't make no sense. I gotta step outside." Byron walked outside to the backyard. Through the open blinds, I saw him lighting a cigarette.

Honey began to sob. Rae and I flanked her sides. She held onto us for dear life.

———

Later that night, in my bed, a small trickle of tears came, to my relief. I had begun to think maybe I was a heartless robot because I couldn't cry. The tears were triggered by the sight of Allan's headphones perched on his nightstand. Those black cushioned circles were his constant companions.

I reached across the bed and grabbed them. Smelled them. Sure enough, the scent of Allan's facial soap came through. Finally, I was able to feel something. *Thank You, God.*

It occurred to me to pray. I simply didn't have the

words, though. "God. You know," was all I could mutter.

Strengthened with the knowledge of His presence, I decided to go ahead and address at least some of the messages and texts in my phone. I followed the charging cord to the bottom drawer of my nightstand and retrieved the phone from where Celeste must have put it.

I had fourteen text messages. The first ones inquired if Allan had really died. I didn't even reply. By now, they had to know. The last bunch of texters let me know they were praying for me. I sent them all the same "Thank You" meme.

There were also twelve voice messages, which probably consumed all the extra space in my phone's memory. Something in me was still hoping to hear a message from Allan saying that he was sorry for leaving the camp without telling me. Maybe he was in a celebrity rehab, or driving cross country in an RV trying to find himself, or maybe someone had kidnapped him. Anything was better than dead.

I didn't have the strength to call anyone back, so I responded to voice messages with generic texts, too.

Celeste had called, but didn't require a response. She just wanted me to know she was praying for me.

The last voice mail message was from Detective Jackson at 7:42 p.m. "Mrs. Crandall, I know you must be busy with family and all. Making final arrangements. That's certainly understandable. Just wanted you to know that the news has gotten wind of the story. You might see some things on television, given your husband's popularity and all. Everything they're reporting is speculation at this point. Give me a call first thing in the morning to touch bases. And don't forget to call me if anything develops on your end."

I regretted that I'd missed his call. Celeste meant well by turning off my phone, but I couldn't afford to let that happen again. I put my phone back in receiving mode.

I didn't even attempt to go into my email account, but I did shoot a message over to the person I figured could put me in touch with Jerry Albright.

With Allan's headphones pressed firmly against my chest, I fell asleep.

I couldn't have been asleep more than half an hour when my phone dinged with a text.

Surely people know not to harass me all night long.

I rolled over and reached my phone. My eyes squinted to focus and read the text from a number that wasn't saved in my system.

Unknown texter: *You didn't have to kill him. We broke up.*

5

I blinked a few times and read the message again. I texted back: *Who is this?*

Unknown texter: *Jonna.*

The name registered. Allan had spoken of her. She was one of the newer weekend DJs at KRBF.

I had a good mind to call her and give her a few choice words from my lips instead of my thumbs. Yet, I wanted the conversation in writing so I could pass it on to Detective Jackson, because this was definitely out of the ordinary.

I sat up in bed and typed: *What do you mean you broke up?*

Jonna: *Exactly what I said. We broke up. Friday night @ retreat place. You killed him for nothing!!!!!!!!!!!!*

I mumbled to myself, "No, I didn't kill *him*, but I'm about to kill *you*, Jonna!"

I texted back: I *did not kill my husband. Maybe YOU did!*

I waited for her to respond. When she didn't reply after five minutes, I called Detective Jackson.

"Hello?"

"Detective Jackson, it's Ashley Crandall. My husband, Allan Crandall...the one from the camp...who died," I forced myself to say. I took a deep breath. "You told me to call if anything unusual happened."

"What's going on?"

"I got a text from a woman. Jonna. She said that she and Allan"—I couldn't believe what I was about to say—"had just broken up. Friday night."

"Were you aware of an affair?"

"No. This is all news to me. I don't even know if it's true."

"Thank you for calling, Mrs. Crandall. This is definitely important information. I must tell you that I had already been alerted to this possibility."

"What?"

"Nothing's confirmed. Can you give me Jonna's number? Let me make a few phone calls tonight. Will I see you first thing in the morning at the station?"

"Yes. Eight o'clock?"

"Promptly," he said it like a command. "Good night."

"Night."

There was nothing *good* about that night, as far as I was concerned. My husband was dead. His self-professed former mistress had accused me of killing him. And the police were holding back information.

No, there was nothing good about that evening.

I put Allan's headphones back on his nightstand.

There was no rest for my eyes, or my heart, between talking to the detective by phone and the moment I'd see him face-to-face. How could I sleep with all that craziness floating around in my head?

———

The next morning, Rae was the only one up before me. She already had the coffee pot going. I quickly grabbed a granola bar from the pantry and my purse from the back of an island chair. "I've got to go meet the detective this morning."

"Don't you want someone to go with you? Celeste called my phone. She said she was getting off at seven this morning and could come by. I'm sure she wouldn't mind going with you."

"No. Tell her not to bother. She just got off a twelve-hour shift."

"Are you going to see Allan's body?"

I shushed my sister. "I don't know, exactly."

Rae peered at me. "What's wrong, Ash?"

47

"Just…some things aren't adding up. I need to talk to the detective. Alone."

"Are you sure?"

"Yes. And stop acting like you're the big sister."

"I'm just sayin', I got your back." She jerked her neck to either side as though preparing for a boxing match.

"Well, stall for me, okay? Make up some kind of excuse for me being gone."

"You want me to lie?"

"Do you have any idea how many times I lied for you during your buck wild days?" I refreshed her memory.

"Why must you go there?"

I laughed. "No. Seriously. If they ask you where I went, just tell them I had to go handle some of Allan's business. I shouldn't be gone too long."

"Got it," she agreed. "Oh! A few things. I called your job and told them about Allan. They sent condolences and said take all the time you need." She tapped her index finger.

"Okay."

Rae tapped her middle finger. "The people from Peaceful Days called. They also sent a huge plant. I put it in the back den."

"Okay. Keep holdin' it down, sis. I appreciate you."

"No problem."

With Rae's blessing, I snuck out of my own house and arrived at the police station a little before eight the next morning. The gray concrete of the city's municipal building seemed to fit the somber mood most people would be in upon approaching the building to bail someone out of jail, file paperwork, pick up records, or pay an overdue bill. There were two people already waiting at the main doors. I waited until one minute after eight, when one of them yanked on the door and walked inside.

I grabbed my purse from the passenger's seat and walked up the sidewalk, then the steps to the police office. A uniformed man behind protective glass asked why I was there.

"I need to see Detective Jackson." I showed the card. "He's expecting me."

After showing my identification and signing in, the officer finally got on the phone and called Detective Jackson. He showed up a few moments later, greeted me, then led me past the secured doors, through a maze of cubicles, and into his spacious corner office.

I took some comfort in the idea that he must have been an experienced officer to have such a large office.

"When can I see my husband's body?"

"As soon as we're finished here. Uh, let me cut to the chase, Mrs. Crandall. We've been talking to some of the men who attended the conference with your husband."

I sat up straight on the edge of my seat. "Yes?"

"It seems that Friday night, sometime after the service, your husband sort of broke rank, left his cabin, and met up with a female in the main parking lot. They spoke. Some of the men thought that, by the tone of the discussion, Allan was talking to his wife. But apparently, that woman was not you. Correct?"

"Correct." *So Jonna wasn't lying.* "Did you talk to Jonna?"

"We have spoken to her. She did, in fact, admit to seeing Allan Friday night. Briefly. She says Allan suspected that you knew about their relationship."

"Is that what she called it—a relationship?"

"They'd only gone out a few times after work. Talked and texted mostly, according to Jonna. Sounds like Allan might have called it off before things got too serious."

Going out after work and communication about anything other than business with Jonna was already too serious in my book.

The detective seemed to be studying my body language for cues.

I sat up even straighter. Put on my poker face.

"Mrs. Crandall, did you have any idea that your husband might have been seeing someone else?"

"No, I did not."

"Because if you did, and you got angry, and you went to talk to him Saturday and the conversation didn't go well, that would be totally understandable." He painted the scenario.

"I did *not* know my husband was cheating, I did *not* kill my husband, and I *don't* appreciate you suggesting otherwise."

I'd seen enough crime TV shows to know that I needed to shut my mouth. "I'm not saying another word to you without an attorney. Am I free to leave?"

"Yes, ma'am. You are."

I hightailed it out of the police station, tears streaming down my face. For as much as I wanted to see Allan's body, I could just imagine how they might use video footage of my uncommon reaction—saturated by anger at this other-woman foolishness—when I finally did see Allan's body. Assuming the detective was even telling the truth, I had no idea how I would react. I needed to be able to see my husband without the threat of whatever I said or did being used against me.

I mumbled on the way to the car. "This is a fine mess you've left for me, Allan. Now I needed a stupid attorney to prove I didn't kill you."

This was the last thing I needed to have going on, given my history with Allan's family. They never quite accepted me. Partly because I'm bi-racial, and partly because I "stole" Allan from everybody in Chester-field. Having Corey had softened things with his family a bit, but given how quickly Byron had turned on me because of the Facebook posts, this thing could get ugly real fast.

That was reason number two that I couldn't tell them about my conversation with the detective. Reason number one: Call me crazy, but I didn't want my husband's reputation tainted with this news of a mistress. He would have been so embarrassed for his family to learn something like that about him.

I was angry with him, but I didn't want everyone else mad at him, too.

———

Byron and Honey were sitting at the kitchen table, still eating Rae's delicious breakfast of sausage, eggs, and French toast.

"Glad you made it back," Honey said.

"It's quite a ways to the nearest Target," Rae said. "They're the only ones who carry the brand of nasal spray I like to use. You can go put it in the room for me, Ash."

Just like old times. I said, "Okay," and walked to the guest room as though I were putting something away for her.

When I returned, Rae had a plate made for me.

She told me to sit down and try to eat a few bites. "You can't run on fumes, you know."

"I'll try."

Honey informed me, "I talked to Cousin Lester last night. He says his funeral home can handle all the arrangements if you're okay with us burying Allan back in Chesterfield."

"That's fine," I agreed quickly. I really didn't care where we buried Allan at that moment. I was still stuck on the thought of him being with another woman just a few days earlier.

Rae caught my gaze, her eyebrow raised. "I thought Allan wanted to be buried next to Corey."

"Right," Byron said thoughtfully, "that makes sense."

"No. I can't plan another funeral right now," I said.

Honey and Byron looked at me suspiciously, so I added, "I just went through this two years ago. Go ahead and let Lester's funeral home handle things."

"Well, if my son wanted to be by his son, we should honor his wishes," Honey insisted.

Your son didn't want to honor his vow to be by his wife. I sighed. "Can Lester do the funeral in Chesterfield and bury Allan here?"

"I suppose," Honey said. "Gonna cost more. Allan had life insurance, didn't he?"

"Of course."

Honey's neck rolled back. "Well, you ain't have to say it like that, Miss Thang."

Rae intervened. "Hey. That's what we're not gonna have. We're all bereaved right now. Let's keep it calm."

Byron said, "I'll call Cousin Lester."

"Good idea," Rae agreed.

"I'm going to bed. I think I'm finally getting sleepy." The drive back had given me a clue that though my emotions were running high, my body was running low.

"Take a few bites before you go," my sister demanded.

I didn't have the energy to fight with her, so I obeyed, then dismissed myself from the table.

I didn't bother undressing. I slipped off my shoes, put my purse down, and lay diagonal across the comforter. Thanks to my position, I came face-to-face with Allan's headphones again.

Stupid old headphones.

Allan, how could you do this to me? After all the praying I had done to save our marriage. Reading books, buying sexy lingerie, going to all those women's conferences trying to learn how to be the consummate wife. My dreams of us ministering together, helping other couples, maybe even starting our own church...utterly ridiculous. I was just hopin' and prayin' and standin' on Scriptures, pleading with

God over Allan's soul, rebuking the enemy, and all this time he was actin' like the enemy! All the meals I had skipped, fasting and trying to get him to Jesus, and there he was trying to get to Jonna! *You really made a fool of me, Allan Derrick Crandall.*

And a lot of good all that praying had done, too —*NOT.* It was bad enough that Allan had let me down. So had God.

I grabbed those headphones and threw them into his closet.

6

Tuesday morning found me back at the police station. This time to meet with the coroner. Upon the advice of the attorney I'd retained, Jessica Clarkson, it was perfectly fine for me to sign the paperwork to have Allan's body transferred to the funeral home. The reports had already been written, his death certificate was available.

The coroner gave me the immediate findings in a written report, which I took with me to the restroom and read in its entirety inside a bathroom stall. As it turned out, a full autopsy wasn't even necessary. Upon removal of Allan's clothing, the cause of death was immediately visible. From the middle of his torso on down to around mid-thigh had suffered blunt force trauma. The report didn't speculate on how Allan had come to be pummeled right in the middle of his body, but apparently he had hit something—or something had hit him—with great force.

I pulled a string of toilet tissue from the roll and sat, crying, for Allan. Who did this to my husband? Did he suffer? Why would someone want him dead? Was it an accident after all?

My mind raced again, almost as quickly as my feet scurried to the car. *Allan is dead*. The paperwork proved it. This was getting more real by the moment.

The cool spring winds brushed against my face. This is really happening.

I didn't want to run into anyone from Detective Jackson's side of the city government building, so I exited through the north doors. He wasn't my friend anymore, clearly. The only way I would find out what happened to Allan was to clear my name so that Jackson wouldn't think he needed to withhold information from me. *Whatever happened to innocent until proven guilty?*

"Excuse me," a man dressed in jeans and a Lakers shirt said to me as I opened my car door.

"Yes?"

"Are you DJ Pistol Whip's wife?"

"Yes. My name is Ashley. My husband's name is Allan." I figured he must have been a distraught fan, the last type of person I wanted to see.

"I'm Robert. I just left the detective's office, giving them more details. I was at the retreat with your husband. I'm so sorry about what happened to him."

"Thank you," I said, wiping a tear away. I hadn't even realized I was still crying from the restroom.

"My son listens to the station all the time," Robert continued. "Against my wishes, sometimes."

Mine too, I wanted to say. "I'm glad he enjoyed my husband's work."

"Um...I don't know if anyone from the retreat has called you. But I wanted you to know that your husband got a lot out of the weekend. You could ask anyone there—he shared a lot. Opened up to us. Opened up to the Lord, too."

I stared at Robert. "What are you doing here at the police station?"

"Detective Jackson called in several of us to follow up on what happened."

For once, I had someone talking to me who wasn't also sizing me up for murder. "So, let me ask you... what really happened to my husband? What happened Friday night, and Saturday?"

Robert shrugged. "Friday night, he was active in the group. Talked about his hopes and fears. How he loved you, but he was messing up his marriage. The death of his son. He really broke down. We surrounded him and prayed for him. Then, his room-mates said he got on his phone later that night. Went out to the parking lot and was talking to someone."

"A woman?" I asked.

"Yes. Well, that's what other dudes were saying—I didn't see her for myself. My room was on the other side of the building."

I swallowed. "And then?"

"That was it for Friday. He came back to his room, went to sleep like everyone else. Saturday, we had chapel, small group sessions. A call to Christ. Your husband answered that call, Ashley. He joined us at the banquet table and gave his life to the Lord."

As Robert spoke, my mind tried to picture this scene: My husband surrendering to God. Surrendering to His will, His plans.

It was almost unbelievable, given the argument we'd had just before I dropped him off.

Robert's smile helped me imagine how beautiful it must have been. "I can't tell you how happy we all were that night. I was like—man, this guy with so much influence in the community was joining us in the Kingdom's agenda. Half the people there already knew who DJ Pistol Whip was, so it was cool. I, for one, was looking forward to his impact.

"Saturday night, they say he kind of did the same thing. He made a phone call, then went outside to meet somebody. We all kind of knew the guidelines— about what time we were supposed to be in the rooms. But we're all grown men. Nobody was going to tell anybody what to do or when to do it. His roomies said he didn't come back after that meeting. The next morning, that's when I found out Allan was dead. I was like—whoa! That was a major blow to us all."

My head bowed, all I could do was shake my head. "Allan sooooo didn't want to go there this weekend."

"It was absolutely the best thing that could have happened to him before he died," Robert said matter-of-factly.

"Thank you, Robert, for letting me know."

"I'm surprised no one had already told you," he said.

"Well, Detective Jackson isn't really trying to put me in touch with people right now. It's a long story. One that I hope will end soon."

"I'll be praying for your comfort and peace," Robert offered.

"Thank you."

I got back into my car, but didn't turn on the ignition immediately. Robert's words hung in my heart, right next to the hole created by Allan's absence.

Wow. It didn't seem fair that God would save Allan and then take him away from me so quickly. What's the point of that?

The only person who could probably help me make sense of things was Celeste. I texted her and asked if she was available and wouldn't mind me stopping by her apartment for a few minutes.

No problem.

Her complex wasn't far from the government offices, so I made it there in fifteen minutes. Celeste opened her door and pulled me into a hearty hug. "Oh honey, I've been praying for you like you wouldn't believe. Rae says you've hardly cried. I was planning to come see you before my shift tonight."

"I've cried, but not for the reasons anyone thinks I'd be crying."

Celeste's brow furrowed. "Come on in."

She sat me down in her kitchen nook and offered some coffee.

I noticed her fully made-up face, which wasn't like her. "Ummm, are you headed somewhere?"

"Steve and I are going to his uncle's retirement party a little later this afternoon."

"I'm sorry, Celeste. I guess I forgot all about the fact that you have a pretty full life now. I should leave."

"Girl, please." She dismissed my words with a wave. "What's going on?"

Finally, I could let someone know the whole truth. Celeste had almost lived in my home during the months before Corey passed. She had seen me and my house at my worst—the dirty dishes, the dirty laundry, the ring in the tub. She'd done a lot more than what she was required to do through home healthcare.

Plus, she had a forgiving heart. If anyone was up for forgiving Allan for cheating, it was her. I didn't have any reason to hide the dirty details from her.

But before we got into the nitty-gritty, I wanted her opinion on the report. I took the manila envelope containing the preliminary coroner's report from my purse. "These papers say that Allan was hit by something, from his lower torso to mid-thigh. What do you make of it?" I gave the packet to Celeste.

She took a few moments to flip through the papers. Once again, I was glad to have a nurse as a friend.

"I mean, I'm no crime scene investigator, but these notes tell me that something slammed into him on his right side. I know Allan, how tall he was and everything. Looks to me, by the diagram, that someone hit him with the front of a car. The front grill of an SUV, given the height and span of the internal injury field."

"That must be why they were looking at my vehicle." I thought out loud.

"Who?"

"The detective and the officer. Sunday, when they left the house, they took pictures of the front of my car."

She set the papers on the coffee table. "Ashley, I don't mean to scare you, but you need a lawyer. From the tone of the conversation the detective had with me when he called to verify your whereabouts, you're not above suspicion."

"Oh, yeah. I forgot to tell you they were going to call."

"No problem. I answered their questions. I even sent them a picture of the receipt through my phone."

"Good. Thanks. This whole thing is crazy. And I'm already on it with the lawyer."

"Okay, that's good. I know officers mean well, but sometimes when they get it in their minds that a certain person is guilty, they lose objectivity," she explained, setting the papers on the table.

"Right."

"Now for the rest. Do you want the good news or the bad news first?" I braced her.

"I don't know what could be much worse than what you're already going through, so let's start with the bad news."

I breathed in deeply through my nose, then exhaled through my mouth. I sat up straight. "Here goes. Allan might have had a girlfriend. Probably."

Celeste didn't flinch.

"Didn't you hear me?"

"Yes. I did."

I bugged my eyes out at her. "Doesn't that come as a surprise to you?"

She rolled her lips between her teeth. "I mean... it's possible that any man could have a weakness."

My shoulders slumped. "What? You think Allan was *capable* of having an affair?"

"He is a human being," she stated, "and we're all *capable* of making bad choices."

"Whoa." I put my hand on my forehead as though checking myself for fever. Celeste's lack of shock. Her calm demeanor. It wasn't adding up. "Soooo...you knew something?"

"I-I mean, just little things. Little signs, but there was never any solid proof of—"

"Signs like what?" I stood, flailing my arms beside me in a desperate plea for answers.

"Ashley," she said calmly, "I am not going to dredge through stuff from years ago. It was all just... suspicion anyway. Allan is a local celebrity. He's a DJ, which is almost like a man who can actually sing. Women must have thrown themselves at him all the time."

I stood and put my hands on my hips, towering over her. "You're telling me you knew my husband was cheating on me when Corey was alive?"

Celeste stood, too. "No, I'm not saying I *knew* anything. Which is why I never *said* anything. I don't get involved in people's marriages."

"But you were my *friend*," I fussed.

"Which is exactly why I didn't say anything," she

said, trying to convince me. "Whatever problems you and Allan had weren't my business. I was your friend. I was Corey's nurse, and I loved your family. The last thing I wanted to do was break it up."

I barked, "So, basically, you would let me live a lie?"

"What? Did you want me to tell you every time I found a number in his pocket?"

"Uh—yes! Wait a minute—how many numbers did you find?"

She gritted her teeth. "If you must know. Two. And I sort of confronted him about the last one. He laughed and threw the number in the trash. He said the girl was someone who was somebody trying to get close to him so she could get a record deal with the former rapper turned producer who was coming to his show the next day. I had to give Allan the benefit of the doubt, especially given the industry he's in."

I closed my eyes because I couldn't even look at her anymore. "I cannot believe this. You're making excuses for him."

Her hands gripped my shoulders.

"Ashley. Open your eyes."

I parted them slightly, wishing these last two days would just disappear completely from my life. My husband was dead. Now, come to find out, Celeste knew more about Allan than *I* did.

"Listen to me. Allan loved you." Her eyes watered.

"He wasn't perfect, but I believe he loved to the best of his ability."

"You know this is absurd, right! Do you hear yourself talking? Really, how would you feel if I told you that, two years ago, I saw Steve at a strip club?"

Celeste squinted. "Ummm...why would you be at a strip club?"

"Why would *Steve* be at a strip club?" I quizzed.

"That makes no sense."

"You know what I mean." I fumed. "You don't get it. I don't expect you to since you're not even married. Maybe when you become a wife and find out that your husband has been collecting women's phone numbers and one of your closest friends didn't bother to tell you, you'll understand."

"Look. I know you're upset. I don't blame you. But let's not speak words we'll later regret," Celeste said in a low tone. "You're in the middle of one of the worst seasons—"

"I don't wanna hear any church talk about season or wilderness or joy coming in the morning! You can save all that for someone else!" I yanked my purse from off the back of a bar chair and stormed to the front door. I fiddled with the two locks while Celeste followed me, pleading with me to stay and listen. I wasn't having it. Finally, I got the locks in the correct position and the door opened.

I left without even saying goodbye. How could I?

How could *she* sit there and go out to dinner with me, and pray for me and my family and my marriage knowing how naïve I was?

The tears tumbled over my eyelids as I drove home. How could I have been so foolish? All those nights Allan claimed to be at a party on behalf of the radio station—was he really living it up with other women? So what if he faced more temptation than the average man. He also got paid to go to parties and live it up in the city. How many men get to do that for a living? He should have known better than to mix business with pleasure.

And who were these chicks anyway? Why were they so desperate? Though I hadn't gone out to many parties with Allan, everybody knew he was married. In all of the pictures that he was tagged in, he was wearing a wedding band. I could say for sure, he never hid his ring.

But Celeste. That was another case altogether. One more betrayal to add to the list. I was almost upset that God had allegedly saved Allan because I didn't think he deserved it.

I turned on the radio. Switched from the gospel station to yesteryear rap because I wasn't in the mood to be holy. DMX came to my rescue that day. I rolled down the windows and threw up all kinds of fake gang signs as I yelled the lyrics to *Lose My Mind*. "Up in here! Up in here!" That music, my anger, and my pain made me want to just fight somebody.

But who was I kidding? I hadn't fought anybody since I was 11 years old. Rae actually won the fight, and she was two years younger than me. The best I could do at the moment was blow my horn at the person in front of me, who'd gotten into my lane a little too quickly. And the only reason I did that was because I could see her silvery gray hair above the headrest.

The radio panel inside my car showed an incoming call, and the ring followed moments later.

"Hey, Rae."

"How did it go with the coroner?"

"Fine." I tried to make my voice sound normal because I still wasn't ready to go into all the particulars.

"Did you see Allan's body?"

"No. I just took the paperwork and left."

"Ash, you can't keep avoiding this. You have to look at him. For closure."

"I know. I'm not ready." I decided to change the subject. "I stopped by Celeste's after. She thinks a vehicle struck him."

"Oh wow. That's crazy."

"I know." I agreed. "You'd think they could look at tire tracks or something to piece together the type of car that was there. As much as we pay for tires, I shouldn't even be a suspect."

"What?" Rae yelled.

I slapped my own cheek.

"What do you mean? Are they trying to nail this on you?" Rae raged.

"No. Not exactly. But I'm not above suspicion."

"What possible motive would you have for killing your own husband?" my sister questioned.

I couldn't answer. "Rae, just...don't worry about it. Everything's going to work out. I trust that the person who did this will be caught."

"They'd better be, or I'll have to go ballistic on somebody. You've been through enough tragedy for, like, five lifetimes in these past two years alone."

"Amen to that."

"By the way, Byron and Honey left. They took some of Allan's clothes back to Chesterfield. Did you sign for the coroner to release the body to their cousin's funeral home?"

"Yes. That was the first thing I did when I got to the city morgue," I said. Though much of the morning still seemed to be a fog, I surprised myself with the ability to recall bits of information.

"Okay. The funeral plans seem to be underway. We should head to Chesterfield, probably. They'll have Allan's body by then. You can see him in a nice suit and everything. That will be good."

Rae was doing her best to prepare me for the inevitable. She had gotten into the habit of this, actually. The last couple of times I went home, she warned me what to expect with Mom. "She might not remember you right away," Rae had told me last year. I didn't believe her, but she'd been right. Mom thought I was my older cousin, Rhonda.

Three months ago, Rae informed me that Mom would probably ask me the same questions in perpetuity. "Just answer them as though it's her first time asking. Don't try to remind her that you've already had this discussion, you'll only agitate her."

And, sure enough, Mom asked me who made the cornbread twelve times at Easter dinner. I counted. Twelve.

"Don't worry, Rae. I've got a lawyer already. We're going to get to the bottom of it. I'm coming home now. What time do you want to leave for Chesterfield?"

"I was planning to run to the gym for a few hours. Your in-laws nearly made me throw 'em out. Byron left at least twenty hairs in the guest bathroom sink this morning. Nasty!"

I laughed. "Allan was worse."

"Oh my gosh." She sighed. "Miss Honey must have been slacking on training her sons how to clean."

Rae had a knack for helping me through the

unthinkable. I really didn't like the fact that all these other people seemed to bc keeping me posted about my own life. Supporting me. Surrounding me like I was helpless. I used to be in control of things. I had an hourly calendar, a week-at-a-glance calendar. I had a 1200-calorie-a-day diet, a regular exercise schedule. I dealt with numbers and calculations and pretty reliable predictions all day.

Then life happened. Times two. Times three, if I ended up in some long, drawn out trial to prove my innocence. *What if I'm found guilty by circumstantial evidence? What if the trial drags on for months? What if I'm in jail when my mother passes away?*

I would definitely need some more DMX music by day and the Bible by night if I was going to jail. "Up in here! Up in here!"

7

Thankfully, my driveway was empty when I returned home. That meant Allan's family was gone. Rae would probably be at the gym for a while. I had the house to myself. Finally. A moment to be treasured. If Allan's death was anything like Corey's, there was no telling how many people from the community, the radio station, and the family would be dropping by over the next several days bringing food, and cards, and plants.

My phone rang again. This time I recognized Detective Jackson's number. I needed to answer so that I could give him my lawyer's contact information. "Hello?"

"Mrs. Crandall."

"Yes."

"Would it be okay if I came by your home? I've got a few follow-up questions to ask."

"No. It's not okay," I answered with a rude twang, still pumped from my rap hangover.

"We can do this the hard way or the easy way."

"What? I need you to—"

"Your brother-in-law called me."

Frozen, all I could do was listen.

"He said that he and Allan's mother were looking through Allan's closet for burial clothing. They found his headphones. The headphones he *always* wore. And they were cracked."

Of course, I had a simple explanation. They were cracked because I threw them into the closet in a fit of anger. I started to share this information, but I didn't want to have my words twisted. "My lawyer will be calling you very soon."

"Yeah. Tell him to call me *very* soon."

"I'll tell *her* to call you ASAP so you can stop calling me."

I hung up, immediately called Jessica, and filled her in on my brief conversation with the detective.

"You did the right thing by not answering his question," she said. "We need to have those headphones examined by our team. They'll be able to show that the impact from you throwing them was nothing compared to whatever hit Allan."

Relief coursed through me.

"Thank you."

"I'll have someone come by later today to pick up the evidence," she said.

"But the police want the headphones. If I give them to you, won't that look like I'm trying to hide something?"

"Until they have a warrant to seize those headphones from your home, they belong to you, and you can do whatever you want to do with them. They can examine them *after* we do. The fact that this detective alerted you to a piece of crucial evidence before he showed up at your doorstep says he's pretty lazy. He thought you'd fold and confess because he thinks you killed Allan. And because he thinks you're the killer, he's not even following up on *real* leads that are probably sitting right under his nose."

This was turning into one of those dramatic lawyer TV shows. "Okay. Gotcha. I'll have the headphones ready."

I thought about leaving the headphones on the floor in the closet and letting the attorney's people do whatever they do—pick them up with plastic tongs, seal them in a plastic bag. But seeing as my in-laws had probably already touched them, it didn't seem to matter.

I did the honors instead, placing the headphones on the small half-table in the foyer so I could give them to the courier right away.

Fifteen minutes later, the bell rang. I swung the door open, expecting to find a man dressed in all black. Instead, there stood my husband's new business partner, Michael Rivers.

"Oh. Hi, Michael. How are you?"

"I'm good. I just...I can't believe it," he said, his mouth wide open in disbelief.

"Me, either."

"Mmmm." He swallowed. "Owning this station was a big dream come true for both of us. I don't know how I'm gonna do it without him."

I wasn't in the habit of letting men in when my husband wasn't home, so I wasn't going to let him inside. "I'm so sorry, but I'm headed out, actually. Busy making arrangements."

"No. Yeah, I understand," he said. His feet respectfully stayed on my outdoor Welcome mat. "I was just dropping by to express my condolences. Your brother-in-law told the station manager that you all are planning to have the funeral in Allan's hometown. KRBF was thinking of planning a memorial here in Dallas. If that's okay with you."

"Sure. No problem. Just let me know when and where. I'll be there," I assured him. *Just don't sit me next to Jonna.* "Do you have my direct number?"

"Yeah. I'm pretty sure I do. Allan made sure everyone knew about you. You were, like, his everything."

I bit my tongue. Literally. What did Michael know about Jonna? About other women? "Did you, by chance, know anything about Allan's, um, female friends?"

Michael's mouth fell open. "Uh...b...naw. I mean...pshhhh...you know, I don't—"

I gave him a hand signal to stop. "Never mind."

"Me and Allan were all about business. That's the only reason I went to see him at the camp Saturday."

"Oh. You talked to him Saturday?"

"Yeah. The detectives said I was one of the last people to see him alive. Didn't they tell you?"

"No." I pushed air through my teeth. "They're not really telling me much of anything right now. What did you and Allan talk about?"

"You know how it is—last minute stuff. I needed him to sign some documents, like pronto. He told me to come through the camp real quick. He signed 'em. We talked for a second about some last minute hiccups in the contract. Man, I never dreamed that would be the last time I saw him." Michael looked up at my doorframe as though the wood could give him answers.

My brain was working double-time, trying to figure out why Jackson didn't want me to know that my husband had seen Michael in his last moments. Then I remembered that the police were trying to frame me—and me alone—for my husband's death.

Michael continued, "Yeah. We said our goodbyes. He walked away. Slipped those good old standby headphones on his ears, and that was the last I saw of him."

"But Allan left his headphones with..." I suddenly realized I'd said too much. And I was already pointing at the headphones.

My eyes popped open with the realization.

Michael's eyes narrowed with evil.

I tried to slam the door. Too late.

Michael pushed his way into my home. He closed and dead-bolted the door with one hand, put his hand over my mouth, seemingly all in one move. My backside was against the wall in a second's time.

"Shut up. Shut! Up!" he ordered. "You're the reason I had to kill Allan anyway!"

A little scream escaped my throat. *What was he talking about?*

"*You* got him brainwashed. Sent him to that church meeting. He's the one who wanted to meet with me Saturday night. And do you know what he wanted? Huh?" Michael screamed in my face.

Even if I had been able to answer, my words would have gotten muffled by his hand.

"He wanted out. Out of our deal. Out of the contract. Said he wanted to do something different with his life. He was *changing*. But that sudden change was gonna cost me a whole lotta money. Told me I had to buy him out," Michael raged. "He blew *my* dreams up in smoke."

I felt no pain. I really didn't feel much fear, either. I wanted to punch him probably as much as he wanted to punch me.

You killed Allan! I bit the inside of his hand like it was a T-bone steak. He yowled, yanking it away from me. We scrambled, fell, and scruffed across the foyer floor, breaking a lamp and a vase along the way.

Crash! Boom!

Michael's hand caught my ankle just before I was able to reach my phone. I kicked his face so hard, I was sure I broke his nose. That gave me just enough head start to make it to my bedroom and lock the door. My adrenaline was pumping so hard I couldn't even see straight. *What do I do? What do I do?* Our windows were too high to climb out of or even signal from. The safety precautions I had made for myself when I was having the house built as a single woman had now become a trap.

"I'm coming in there," Michael warned as he pounded against my doorframe. "Don't make this ugly."

"Get out!" I screamed. I wished we'd owned a gun, or a knife, or something. For all that gangsta rap DJ Pistol Whip played, my husband didn't have one single firearm in the house. "You're not going to get away with anything!"

The pounding continued. My door was starting to come off its hinge. My soul knew that Michael had every intention of killing me.

"Please, God," I prayed as I crouched on the side of my bed. "Please don't let him kill me."

Suddenly, I heard a crack, a thud, a grunt, and a scream coming from the other side of my door. There was someone else in the house.

Did Michael bring someone with him?

"You all right, baby?" a male voice asked.

Baby?

I jumped with the next round of beating on my door. "Ashley! Ashley!"

"Celeste! I'm in here!"

The door handle rattled. "Open the door, Ashley. It's okay."

My feet wouldn't move. My body wouldn't move. "I can't."

"Are you hurt?"

"No. I don't think so."

"Okay, then you can do this. You can get up and open the door, honey. Come on. Open the door."

Wait a minute. Maybe Celeste and Michael killed Allan together.

"You want us to come in and get you?" the male voice asked. It was much deeper than Michael's voice.

"Who are you?"

"Steve."

"Where's Michael?"

"On the floor. Knocked out," Steve answered.

Unless all three of them were in on Allan's death, I was safe. I crawled to the door and unlocked it. Celeste opened it and rushed in while Steve called 9-1-1. She quickly sank to her knees and held me. "My God! Ashley, you left the coroner's paperwork at my apartment. Thank God we came by to return it to you. I heard you screaming. Used my spare key to come in. Thank God, Steve was with me!"

Celeste squeezed me tightly. "Hallelujah. Thank the Lord," she half-sang and half-cried.

I joined in her thanks when I heard the police sirens.

8

Local media went crazy over Allan's death once they found out that DJ Pistol Whip had been killed by DJ Drop-the-Bomb. Hurtful online memes followed. People who had never even heard of KRBF were posting, blogging, and commenting about the situation as though the entire hip hop world had suffered a tragedy.

Cousin Lester's funeral home got word there was going to be media present at the funeral. Allan's family and I decided that rather than let the world make a circus of my husband's homegoing, we would have a private one instead. Just close family and friends—plus Steve—at the funeral home. I figured since he'd saved my life and punched my husband's killer and all, he could definitely come to Allan's funeral.

We were all grieving so deeply that I didn't have the energy to confront Byron about contacting the police regarding the broken headphones. For all they knew, the mystery might have been solved before the detective accused me.

I didn't tell Rae about the Crandall family suspicions, either, or we would have had another circus on our hands. Some stuff just needs to be left alone to keep down confusion.

I didn't stay in Chesterfield more than a few hours after the service. Rae, Celeste, Steve, and I headed back to the Dallas area following the ceremony. Rae, who had driven my car there and back, said she was pooped so she went to bed almost as soon as we arrived home.

Celeste said she'd stay the night, so Steve dropped her off at my house.

I was glad to have her company. Plus, I owed her an apology. Once we changed into pajamas and took off makeup and hairpieces, we reclined in my family room with my favorite butter pour-over popcorn.

We settled on the couch beside each other.

"What's in your head, sis?" she asked.

"First, I want to tell you I'm sorry."

Celeste frowned. "Sorry for what?"

"Sorry for going off on you about Allan and cheating—"

"Girl, please. I put everything you said that day in file thirteen."

I laughed. "File thirteen? Really?"

"Yes. I have to. I know you were hurting, lashing out at those closest to you. I've seen it all too often in my work. Comes with the territory. Can't take it personally. I've gotten so good, I can forgive someone before they've even had a chance to finish offending me."

I moaned. "That'll come in handy when you get married."

"Right!"

"You ready to walk down the aisle?"

"More than ready." She smiled. "Excited. Blessed. Anxious."

"You're going to be a great wife, Celeste. And a great mother someday, too."

"One step at a time," she fussed.

"I know, I know. But I mean it. You're so full of compassion, and love, and good news. Steve is blessed to have you. Everyone who knows you is blessed to have you in our lives."

"Oh!" Celeste held up her hand. "Speaking of good news. Before the blah-blah-blah at my apartment the other day, you said there was good news about Allan. I never got to hear it. What was it?"

I took a moment to rack my brain. Had I really not talked to Celeste about Allan becoming a believer? A quick replay of that day's events flashed through my mind. She was right. Between talking to the police, running from the media, trying to plan for a private ceremony, and getting myself together for the funeral, I hadn't filled her in.

"Okay, so, I saw one of the guys from the retreat when I was leaving the police station—back when I was still a suspect. Anyway, the guy said Allan became a Christian the night before he died."

Celeste raised her hands in the air. "Hallelujah! Glory to God!" She began to cry right there in the middle of rejoicing.

"I know, I know." I had to agree. "But why is he dead now? I'm the one who fasted and prayed for Allan to get saved. I had big dreams for us—ministering and helping other people. We never got to pray together, go to church together. I just...and with the girlfriend thing...it's hard to reconcile everything."

Celeste grabbed my hands. "Does it really matter what Allan did before he came to Christ?"

I squirmed, admitting my true feelings. "Yeah. It does."

"To you, maybe," she said. "Does it matter to God?"

"Probably not. A slave to sin is a slave to sin. I get that. I just feel...cheated again that I didn't get, like, twenty years to flaunt my Christian husband!"

"Ashley, God didn't save your husband for *you*.

God saved Allan because He loved *Allan*. Now, I don't have an answer for what happened later that evening. I only have the truth, which is that what matters most is knowing your husband will never hear the words 'depart from me.' You will get to see him again in the presence of Jesus. Your prayers for Allan *were* answered. Maybe not for reasons that would make your life easier or to do this whole Christian-couple thing the way you wanted it. But your love for Allan opened his heart to hear the good news. So don't get mad at God. Don't get mad at Allan. I'm sorry he's dead to you right now, but he's never been more alive than he is right now with Christ."

All I could do was tip over onto Celeste and cry, because she was right. Allan was gone, but he wasn't lost. And God *had* answered my prayers in the nick of time.

I couldn't thank God that Allan was dead, but I did thank Him that he was alive. "Thank You, Lord." I joined Celeste in her praises. She held onto me, like a mother rocking a 5-year-old, and I cried all the tears I could.

It felt good to release all the pent-up anxiety and stress with Celeste.

Before she left the next day, she prayed for me, claiming God for the inexplicable peace left to us in His Word.

My prayer for myself was that someday I could be someone else's "Celeste." She was in her mid-thirties, not much older than me. Yet, she was much more stable, spiritually, which she accredited to daily time alone with the Lord, despite her long work hours and grueling schedule.

I had asked her, once, how she managed to squeeze in quiet time with God every day.

"I couldn't make it *without* time alone with Him," she admitted. "Otherwise, the cares of this world and the nature of my work would overtake me."

She was right. I couldn't imagine caring for sick, hurting children day in and day out. Celeste was definitely graced for her job.

―――――

Allan's body was brought back to Dallas for burial next to Corey the following week.

I left the public to do all of their ogling at the memorial put on by Dallas area hip hop artists. I thought they would have cancelled the whole thing, with Michael being charged and in jail. But it must have been good for ratings, so the station carried on. I guess Jonna, or somebody else, picked up the slack. I had no idea and I really didn't care. Those people didn't know Allan, really. At least not the brand-spanking-new Allan in Christ.

I didn't know the new Allan, either, which made things a little awkward for me. Was there even a new Allan anyway?

My question was answered unexpectedly when the police finally gave me all of Allan's belongings that had been confiscated from the camp. Amongst his belongings, I found evidence of the husband I had prayed for, yet never knew. The men had been keeping a weekend journal, writing their deepest thoughts, concerns, failings. Their "notebook" was more like a pamphlet with six boxes for reflection throughout the weekend. Nothing like the endless-lined spiral bound notebooks distributed at women's conference. The planners really knew their audience, I gathered.

Of course, Allan never got the opportunity to write in his sixth box on Sunday morning. But—quite to my surprise—he had participated and written in the other ones.

Friday Afternoon

This is crazy. Can't believe I'm here. Sitting around a campfire. Might as well hold hands and sing Cumbaya. I'm just here for Ashley. She has all these ideas about how things are supposed to be, how we are supposed to live. She should know by now that nothing works out the way you planned. That's life. Take the good and the bad.

Friday Evening

Okay, God. I see. This isn't about Ashley. It isn't even about Corey. It's about me. And You. And Jesus. But it seems like it's mostly about me and You. I hear you.

Saturday Morning

I did it. I ended it. That felt like a ton of weight off my shoulder. God, You know I flirt and blow kisses at the ladies, but I've never done anything like what I think was about to happen. It's like Ice Cube said: Check yourself before you wreck yourself! Only You did the checking. Not me. Thank You.

Saturday Afternoon

That was wild, God! I heard You talking to me. Inside of me. Like You have a rope inside of me and You're pulling me to You. I don't know if I want to come. My lifestyle. My business. My music. You know I love my music! I can't be all sitting up in church every Sunday. Going to a whole bunch of church stuff. Meetings and volunteering. I don't know if I can do all that, God.

Saturday Evening

It's finished. It IS finished. At the Cross and in me. I don't know what it will mean, what it will look like, or exactly what it will cost me to follow You. All I know is: I can't be without You.

The night I read Allan's notes felt almost like the night I said goodbye to Corey. Tears of pain and rejoicing flowed. I'd wondered, back then, how it was possible to be so sad and so full of joy at the same time. It had been heart-wrenching to watch my son suffer. Death was a sweet release for him.

What was death for Allan? Didn't God have work for Allan to do? The speaker at the last conference Celeste invited me to said that God saves us to serve. How could that be when Allan never got a chance to do anything for God?

I lay in bed wondering. Thinking. Thanking God for letting me know what happened—or rather what *didn't* happen—between Allan and Jonna. Asking God questions with Allan's headphones, which still smelled of his scent, right next to my nose.

The scent was fading, though. Rae had gone back to take care of Momma. I was scheduled to start back to work in a few days. Celeste was getting married in a few weeks. Life was moving on, just like it had when Corey died. I didn't want to be stuck again. More than that, I didn't want to start planning for my future, when, clearly, things didn't go according to Ashley Crandall's detailed outline.

If Allan had been there and I'd shared my thoughts with him, he would have told me to relax. I could almost hear him whispering to me, "Listen to some music. That's what I do when I get stressed."

I didn't have a playlist on my phone, but I did have links to songs people sent me every now and then.

Carefully, I slid Allan's headphones onto my head. I flipped the on switch. Despite the crack in the plastic dome, my phone lit up, showing that the connection had been established.

I clicked on a link Celeste had sent me the morning of the funeral. I didn't know the artist, but the words and the melody of this sweet song about God's comfort filled my heart almost instantly. The chorus sang, "It will be all right." I laid across my bed, my head resting on Allan's pillow.

Allan had been right. The music was soothing. And those headphones were amazing!

I had to laugh at myself. At him. At what God had done with us. And I had to admit: there's no better ending to a person's life story than "And he lived happily ever after with the Lord." That's the only line in anybody's life that matters, really.

God had written that for Allan. He had written it for me, too. The rest—this life in between—wasn't always comfortable, or fun, or predictable. But because I knew the end, I could live in peace with God's assurance.

It will be all right.

The End

DISCUSSION QUESTIONS

1. In the opening chapter, Ashley says she is getting to the end of her strategies for how to fix her marriage. Have you ever been at your wit's end when dealing with a person? How did that situation turn out?

2. Do you think Ashley was being judgmental toward Allan's line of work, or did she have a legitimate concern when it came to her husband participating in wet T-shirt contests and twerking competitions? How do you feel about Christians working in jobs that might be perceived as detrimental to others?

3. Ashley doesn't feel as though she can grieve until all her questions are answered. Do you have unanswered questions in your

life? How does faith help you keep moving despite the unknowns?

4. Have you ever lost more than one loved one in a short period of time? How did you make it through the grieving process?

5. Ashley didn't want Allan's family to find out that he might have been having an affair before he died. Did you sympathize with her desire to protect her husband's reputation?

6. Do you think Celeste should have told Ashley about her suspicions about Allan cheating?

7. After Celeste told Ashley about her suspicions, Ashley got in the car and turned on rap music because she was "not in the mood to be holy." She felt like she wanted to just fight somebody. Have you ever felt that way? Is it possible to go in and out of Christianity at will?

PLEASE, PRETTY PLEASE LEAVE A REVIEW!

That's right. I'm begging (LOL)! In case you didn't know, good reviews help boost authors' visibility on in online stores. By writing a review, you help other readers make informed decisions about where to find the best information and entertainment. If this book was a blessing to you, please take a moment to share your experience at your favorite online book retailer.

MORE BOOKS BY MICHELLE STIMPSON

No Weapon Formed – Revisit LaShondra and Stelson ten years after their whirlwind romance. Now married and the parents of two bi-racial children, they must learn to toggle faith and clashing cultures.

The Blended Blessings Series – Angelia didn't get it right with her first marriage. Or her second. She hopes this third time will work out, but with twin step-daughters and a mother-in-law who don't like the status quo, this may be the most difficult marriage yet.

A Forgotten Love – One bad play brought London Whitfield's brief professional football career to a devastating end. Back at home and reluctantly living life as an average Joe, London reconnects with the one girl, Daphne, who represents the best and the worst relationship he ever experienced.

All This Love - Knox Stoneworth got dumped at the altar—literally—and has spent the last few years burying himself in work to move past the pain. After a night of celebrating his parents' anniversary, Knox meets a stranger who just might change his mind about his future.

Married for Five Minutes - Take a 5-minute peek inside real marriages facing challenges that threaten to blur the reflection of Christ that marriage was created to be.

**Michelle has written more than 40 fiction and non-fiction books,
so be sure to check out her author pages at online retail stores!**

ABOUT THE AUTHOR

Michelle Stimpson's works include the highly acclaimed *Boaz Brown*, *Divas of Damascus Road* (National Bestseller), and *Falling Into Grace,* which has been optioned for a movie. She has published several short stories for high school students through her educational publishing company at WeGotta-Read.com.

Michelle serves in women's ministry at Oak Cliff Bible Fellowship in Dallas, TX and Cornerstone Bible Church in Cedar Hill, TX. She regularly speaks at special events and writing workshops sponsored by churches, schools, book clubs, and educational orga-nizations.

The Stimpsons are proud parents of two young adults, grandparents of one super-sweet granddaughter, and the owners of one Cocker Spaniel, Mimi, who loves to watch televangelists.

VISIT MICHELLE ONLINE

www.MichelleStimpson.com

www.facebook.com/MichelleStimpsonWrites

Made in the USA
San Bernardino, CA
24 November 2017